The Bears We Know

Brenda Silsbe · Vlasta van Kampen

annick press

toronto + new york + vancouver

We acknowledge the support of the Canada Council for the Arts, the Ontario Arts Council, and the Government of Canada through the Book Publishing Industry Development Program (BPIDP) for our publishing activities.

 ONTARIO ARTS COUNCIL
CONSEIL DES ARTS DE L'ONTARIO

Cataloging in Publication

Silsbe, Brenda
     The bears we know / Brenda Silsbe, Vlasta van Kampen.

ISBN 978-1-55451-167-9 (bound).—ISBN 978-1-55451-166-2 (pbk.)

     I. Van Kampen, Vlasta.   II. Title.

PS8587.I268B45 2009   jC813'.54   C2008-903914-9

The art in this book was rendered in watercolor.

The text was typeset in Billy Light.

Distributed in Canada by:
Firefly Books Ltd.
66 Leek Crescent
Richmond Hill, ON
L4B 1H1

Published in the U.S.A. by:
Annick Press (U.S.) Ltd.
Distributed in the U.S.A. by:
Firefly Books (U.S.) Inc.
P.O. Box 1338
Ellicott Station
Buffalo, NY 14205

Printed in China.

Visit Annick at: www.annickpress.com

To the original bears, Eric, Brad, Don and Roy. With thanks to Wanda.
—B.S.

For Jan, the love of my life, who shared my laughter as I created each bear scenario.
—V.v.K.

There is a house way at the end of our road.

It is a big brown house with many windows and a long staircase. And this is where the bears live.

We have never seen the bears, but we know they are there. And we know what they do.

They sleep late every day. And nobody ever wakes them up or tells them they are sleeping late.

Because, you know, you never wake up or talk back to bears.

When they get up, they sit on the long windowsill and drink coffee and pick tasty crumbs out of their fur.

They watch everything that goes on and growl whenever anyone gets too close. So no one ever does.

They find old couches at the
dump and bring them home ...

... j^umpⁱng
on them till the
springs are gone.
That's their exercise.

Then the bears close the curtains and watch cartoons and game shows on TV.

They don't go to school and they never have to work.

There are always lots of empty potato chip bags in their garbage cans.

Before lunch, the bears go out to their shack and have a sauna.

They wear very tight bathing suits and sing all the time.

Jo and I heard them singing, so we know.

They were singing about a picnic.

The house is very dirty and the bears never clean it. When it looks too clean, the bears bring in buckets of sawdust and throw it around.

For lunch, the bears have vegetable milkshakes and syrup. Sometimes they make omelets.

Then they stretch out before the fire and have a nap.

After their nap, they make hot buttered toast and hot chocolate.

Then they sing very sad songs and cry.
It is a terrible sound when all the bears cry.

But soon one bear tells a joke or sings a happy song, and they eat some more buttered toast and have a good time.

Most days they stay up very late—
way past our bedtime. So we never
know when they go to bed.

So it goes, day after day.

People ask us how we know so much about the bears when we've never seen them.

Well ... some things you just **know**.